The text of this book is set in Avant Garde. The illustrations are rendered in pastel, ink, and pencil.

Manufactured in Singapore. First edition.

10 9 8 7 6 5 4 3 2 1

Library of Congress Cataloging-in-Publication Data
Ernst, Lisa Campbell. Little Red Riding Hood: a newfangled prairie tale/written and illustrated by Lisa Campbell Ernst. 1st ed. p. cm. Summary: An updated version, set on the prairie, of the familiar story about a little girl, her grandmother, and a not-so-clever wolf. ISBN 0-689-80145-9 [1.Fairy tales. 2.Folklore.] I.Title. PZ8.E7Li 1995 [398.21]—dc20 94-45723

Thanks to Jillian, Sally, and The Ellis School!

LITTLE RED RIDING HOOD

A Newfangled Prairie Tale

LISA CAMPBELL ERNST

Simon & Schuster Books for Young Readers

Once upon a time there was a little girl who lived at the edge of a great prairie. Because she always wore a jacket with a red hood when she rode her bike, everyone called her Little Red Riding Hood.

Now one morning, as Little Red Riding Hood sat eating her favorite wheat berry muffins, she had an idea.

"Mom," she said, "it's going to be a real scorcher today. Grandma sure would love it if I brought her some muffins and lemonade. You know how crabby she gets in the heat." Little Red Riding Hood loved visiting her grandmother.

"Great idea," her mother said.

So Little Red Riding Hood's mother packed the still-warm wheat berry muffins and cold lemonade into a basket.

After airing up the tires on her bike and testing the brakes, Little Red Riding Hood set out on her way.

"Now don't forget," called her mother. "Go straight to Grandma's, and whatever you do, don't talk to strangers."

"Sure, Mom," Little Red Riding Hood promised.

Little Red Riding Hood pedaled down Toad Road, past the gas station, the feed store, and the old Wilson place. She waved at everyone she saw, and everyone waved back.

As the edge of town disappeared, and the prairie began, Little Red Riding Hood zig-zagged between the crops, taking the shortcut to Grandma's house. Blackbirds startled and sunflowers swayed as she whizzed by.

"What a nice visit this will be," Little Red Riding Hood said. "Grandma simply adores muffins and lemonade."

But who should be cutting through that same field — and up to no good, I might add — but a very hungry wolf.

When the smell of those wheat berry muffins came wafting his way, the wolf's nose quivered. "Gadzooks!" he whispered. "What is that scrumptious smell?"

The wolf rushed toward the heavenly odor. "Whatever it is, I must have it," he growled.

With one giant leap, the wolf landed right
in front of Little Red Riding Hood's bicycle.

"A*ha*!" he roared.

Little Red Riding Hood slammed on her
brakes. "Hey! Be careful!" she shouted. "You
could get hurt surprising someone like that!"

The wolf chuckled at the warning. "What's
in the basket, dearie?" he asked with a wide-
toothed grin.

"Muffins and lemonade," Little Red Riding Hood said slowly, "for my grandmother."

"But such a tantalizing smell," the wolf drooled. "They must be *very special* muffins!"

"Oh, they are!" Little Red Riding Hood said proudly. "They're my grandma's secret recipe, and they always take first prize at the fair."

The wolf licked his lips. "She must be a dear, sweet woman," he crooned. "Do you have very far to travel?"

"Oh no," Little Red Riding Hood answered, "just over that ridge, this side of Turkey Creek."

"Mmm-hmm," the wolf smirked, his mouth curling up at the corners. "How fortunate."

"I have to go," Little Red Riding Hood said quickly. "Grandma's waiting."

The wolf slyly turned in the opposite direction and pointed. "Ooooh," he gasped. "What beautiful flowers! Such a dear, sweet grandmother *surely* deserves some of those!"

Little Red Riding Hood nodded. "Gee, you're right," she said, jumping off her bike, "Grandma loves flowers. Do you think she'd like these white ones, too?"

But the whistle of the prairie wind was the only response. The wolf was gone.

Of course the wicked wolf had a dastardly plan. "Hardy-har-har!" he laughed wildly, as he raced through the wheat.

"First I surprise that feeble old granny and steal her recipe. Then I wait for the kid in the red jacket to show up with the treats. Soon *I'll* hold the secret to those delectable muffins, and those two country bumpkins won't know what hit them!"

His evil chuckles drifted through the fields.

When the wolf arrived at Grandma's house, he found a note on the door.

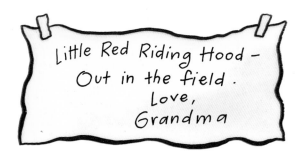

Little Red Riding Hood —
Out in the field.
Love,
Grandma

"This will be easier than I thought!" the wolf snarled. "Grandma's obviously off her rocker, wandering around in the heat. Muddled brains are so easy to persuade!" The wolf cackled, feeling enormously pleased with his good fortune.

But when the wolf searched the fields for Little Red Riding Hood's tottering granny, all he could see was a farmer riding a tractor.

Impatient, he shouted. "Hey! Old man! Where's the ancient granny who lives in the house?"

The farmer, though, seemed to hear nothing. "Very well," the wolf said with a snicker. "I love surprising these dim-witted hicks." And he began to silently sneak up behind the tractor.

Then — before the wolf knew what was happening — the farmer whirled around and grabbed him by his fancy suspenders.

"Hold it right there, scoundrel!" the farmer shouted. "What in tarnation do you think you're doing?"

The wolf gasped and stammered, "I-I-I'm looking for the frail, loony, muffin-baking granny who lives in the house."

"Well, Sherlock!" boomed the farmer, whose grip tightened on the wolf. "*You're talking to her!*"

The wolf's mouth dropped open, and he began to shake. "M-m-my," he finally whispered, "what big *eyes* you have, Grandma."

"All the better to *see* you, skulking around my fields!" Grandma answered.

"My, what big *ears* you have, Grandma," the wolf croaked.

"All the better to *hear* you coming," Grandma answered.

"My, what big *hands* you have, Grandma," the wolf groaned.

"All the better to crush you like a bug, if need be," said Grandma. And, lucky for the wolf, Little Red Riding Hood rolled up just at that moment.

"Grandma, are you OK?" called Little Red
Riding Hood.

"Sure, sweetie," Grandma said.

Together, they marched the grumbling wolf to
Grandma's kitchen, Grandma lecturing all the way.
"Didn't you think if there was a Little Red Riding
Hood there might be a *Big* Red Riding Hood? I
thought I got rid of bullies like you when I moved
away from that forest!

"Might as well have a bite to eat while we
decide what to do next," Grandma said. The wolf for
once was silent, his mouth full of the delicious muffins.

"Of *course*," Grandma said at last.

Soon after, Grandma opened her own muffin shop in town, just west of the post office.

The wolf? He was her chief baker, salesclerk, and dishwasher, being kept much too busy to cause trouble for anyone. Naturally, the wolf got to eat all the muffins he wanted, which improved his disposition enormously.

But just in case he got any ideas about stealing Grandma's recipe again, Grandma always put in the last secret ingredient herself.

Little Red Riding Hood, too, went to work for her grandmother, delivering muffins on her bike.

Every day, rain or shine, the wolf carefully packed Little Red Riding Hood's basket.

"Hey, kid!" he called after her as she whizzed down Toad Road. "Don't talk to strangers!"

And Little Red Riding Hood never did again.